The Keepinnit Reels

Michael Pollick

Published by Michael Pollick, 2024.

THE KEEPINNIT REELS

First edition. June 19, 2024.

Copyright © 2024 Michael Pollick.

ISBN: 979-8227051905

Written by Michael Pollick.

Also by Michael Pollick

Michael Pollick's Proving Ground
Michael Pollick's Proving Ground
The Keepinnit Reels

Table of Contents

PERMANENT RECORDS
DEPARTMENT

IN SEARCH OF: The "Permanent Record."

A former Vulcan once hosted a series of paranormal investigations called IN SEARCH OF, and one topic he managed to miss was the mythical "permanent record." From the first half-day of kindergarten to the final "what am I even doing here?" days as a Senior, school authorities allegedly maintained a secret file on every student's academic ups and downs. Anything and everything you did within the hallowed halls would be dutifully recorded, and would follow you for the rest of your post-graduate life.

The mere threat of adding a minor infraction to this permanent record was enough to keep most of us in line. Teachers delivered the line "This is going on your permanent record, young man!" with absolutely no hint of deception. Part of their job, after we got on the bus, was to compile a daily list of permanent record addendums. Nothing escaped their steadfast gaze, so you'd better be good for goodness sake.

Years later, I discovered that an adult could formally request a copy of the mythical permanent record for a nominal fee. As it turned out, the reality of the permanent record was nothing like the myth. A few test results HERE, a few report cards THERE. Spock didn't even need to get out of his trailer.

Tales From The Great Backyard: The Exact Opposite Of Glamping

Before the arrival of high-end recreational vehicles mounted on semi-truck frames, there were camper shells designed to nest on a sketchy pickup truck. While the Swiss Family Robinson may have found purpose and enlightenment in the Great Outdoors, the Stow Family Pollick mostly added one more thing to the carport. Except for a handful of overnight trips to local fishing holes or campgrounds, our shell away from home stayed tethered to the house with an orange extension umbilical cord.

Perhaps it was because the cushions contained ten times more flame retardant than a cheap Halloween costume, or the concentration of dust and pollen inside the cabin, but these campers brought out the worst in me. One night a friend invited my brother and me over to spend the night in HIS family's camper, and our snacks of choice were cans of Vienna sausages and generic grape soda. Clearly not the breakfast, lunch or dinner of champions.

I don't know how many would-be backyard campers actually made it through the entire night, especially when they turned on the crickets and shut off the heat. We always went out to the campground with the best of intentions, but usually made our way back to our comfortable, warm beds long before our normal breakfasts hit the table.

You Typed Me All Night Long: Heavy Metal And The Home Row

Ordinarily, high school typing classes made watching paint dry sound more inviting. However, my 10th-grade typing instructor found a way to make the time fly by, if only on Fridays. She allowed one lucky student to bring in an album of his or her choice, and it took the place of the standard and exceedingly monotonous typing guide. "J. K. L. Sem." was gleefully replaced by "I can't get no satisfaction" or "Hey, hey, mama, I say the way you move".

We were fortunate enough to be in a mostly abandoned hallway in the oldest part of the school. Most Fridays the album of choice was "Back In Black" by those Australian belters AC/DC. I literally learned to type while listening to the title track, followed by "Hells Bells" and "Givin' The Dog A Bone". Truth be told, I was much more into New Wave at that time, but just being in the same room as those rockers from Down Under was a nice pick-me-up.

I stopped taking formal typing lessons after that class ended, but like the rest of us early Gen Xers, I kept up my chops just in time for the home computer revolution a few years later. It's never been quite the same without the background noise, and to this day whenever I hear "Back In Black" on the radio, my fingers automatically reach for the home row.

Bathrobes, Paper Plates, Tinsel: An Intro To Church Play Stagecraft

An important requirement for church membership is a willingness to mumble at least one line in a church-sponsored Nativity play. It might just be "Lo, I am but a lowly shepherd, and I am sore afraid!" while pointing towards the sky, but it does move the plot. Costume notes include bathrobes, towel turbans, and untamed Halloween costume beards. Continuity is Job 4.

The other cinematic shorthand involves the use of common household items such as paper plates, Christmas tree garlands, and coat hangers. Without the proper divine headgear, it can be hard to pick out the little cherubs from the rest of the crowd. In my hometown, a local factory produced a gold-colored adhesive tape called Mac Tac, and it was overused with abandon.

My brother once assisted with a special effect surrounding the ascension of Jesus. In reality, "Jesus" stood on the in-floor baptistry cover while an amateur weightlifter pressed and locked it above his head. My brother turned on the blacklight. Jesus ascended 18 inches into the heavens.

Trapper Keepers: Organize Your Files, Store Your Supplies, Block Out The Sun

No back-to-school ritual in the 1980s was complete without the selection of a new Trapper Keeper, the embodiment of "everything in its place and a place for everything." Trapper Keepers were designed specifically to hold the company's other product line called Trappers. They featured a wide range of rad graphics, and had the capacity to store everything from paper to pens to rulers. They were also large enough to block out the sun if necessary.

Trapper Keepers filled the void left behind by pencil boxes and loose-leaf binders, but started to buckle under their own weight by the end of the 90s. Storing and carrying an original Trapper Keeper became a skill all its own. One corner or another was always making unsolicited contact with a doorway or an elbow or something. A Trapper Keeper could easily become a Trapper Spiller if held at the wrong angle.

Although leaner, meaner versions of the Trapper Keeper are still on the market, the originals have largely gone the way of Members Only jackets and parachute pants. Those of us who remember should remain most righteous and totally tubular in their honor.

Are You Ready For Some FOOSBALL? The Non-Athletic Thrill Of Youth Group Competition

Friday night was youth night at my childhood church, which happened to be right next door to my house. This meant time was not a factor—I could stay until the last cookie was eaten and the last ping-pong ball rolled away. In the converted tool and die shop we called the youth center, there were three major entertainment options: Ping-Pong, Bumper Pool, and Foosball. To this day, I have no idea what the rules of Bumper Pool actually were.

Foosball was where the action was. While the adults sat around drinking coffee from the avocado green urn and filled up on electrocuted hot dogs, the kids congregated in another room and formed foosball alliances. One-on-one play was an option, but two-person teams provided the sort of high-level play our fans had grown to expect. The biggest concession to safety was the institution of a no-spinning rule, the foosball equivalent of restrictor plates.

Even without spiking privileges, several formidable opponents rose from the ranks, and the rest of us watched in wide-eyed wonder at the display of cat-like reflexes on both sides. At least that's how I would write it up for Sports Illustrated, if they ever asked. Meanwhile, to the victor goes the left-over hot dogs.

Ultraman Is Going To Die, And I Just Can't. I Just Can't.

I can't hold the entire staff at Channel 43 responsible for the near-death of Ultraman, but it was a terrible thing to do to a kid. I should back up. Channel 43 was a local UHF channel originally housed in a renovated bowling alley. They showed the usual selection of children's shows, like Little Rascals and Huckleberry Hound, to more adult fare, like Hee Haw and Star Trek. Two shows in particular caught my ten-year-old fancy, and both came from Japan.

Johnny Sokko and His Flying Robot was straightforward enough. A young boy controls a benevolent giant robot with his wristwatch, and together they fight monsters. The second feature was Ultraman, in which a member of an elite police force can summon the life force of an alien to...well...fight monsters. He's on a timer, however, and a yellow warning light blinks when the battery is low.

In one episode, Ultraman ignored the yellow light completely, causing a previously unknown red light to glow. Ultraman was going to die, and a ten-year-old boy was about to lose his mind. Fortunately for both of us, an even bigger Ultraman swooped down and recharged him. I had to settle for pizza rolls.

In Defense Of NECCO Wafers: I Am But A Small Voice.

CONVENIENTLY TIMED just before Halloween, lists of the worst candies ever created magically appear across the Internet. The lists almost always contain heavy hitters like black licorice, Circus Peanuts, and Peeps. Sometimes those peanut butter chews in orange and brown wrappers will appear, along with Good & Plenties and Dots. I tend to throw Milk Duds under the bus myself.

But there's one perennial member of that group I believe deserves a little more respect and understanding, and of course I'm referring to the original gangsta, NECCO wafers. NECCO wafers have apparently been around since the dawn of Man, or at least the 1830s. These coma-inducing slugs of sugary love were enjoyed by my parents, their parents, their grandparents, and even the ones not covered in the Ancestry subscription. NECCO wafers survived the Civil War, and all other wars after that. Can any of us make the same claim?

NECCO wafers get a bum rap because they are so extremely primal. It's sugar, flavored with whatever herbs were available then, and pressed into bite-size portions for good pioneer children. When you crunch up a NECCO wafer, you're experiencing the same disappointment and cringe as your forefathers, and THAT alone should keep it off the list.

Children's Public Television: Is It Too Late To Be A ZOOM Kid?

While the Big Three networks may have owned Saturday mornings, and local channels featured shows like Captain Kangaroo, Romper Room, and the New Zoo Review, public television managed to win the hearts and minds of "today's young people." Mister Roger's Neighborhood, Sesame Street, and The Electric Company was where it was at, baby. Easy Reader, back me up on that.

Sesame Street held the high ground, with its sometimes frenetic pace and clever blend of human and felt-based characters. From an obsessive-compulsive blue cookie junkie to grocery store owners who should have lived forever, Sesame Street hit just right. The Electric Company was a worthy upgrade, with live-action skits featuring Rita Moreno and Morgan Freeman delivering the linguistic goods without insulting our fledgling intelligence.

The show I really wanted to be on was ZOOM, with an evolving cast of Boston-area kids spending time showing other kids the coolest tricks ever. I still speak fluent Ubby Dubby, and I also do that weird swirly thing with my arms and elbows. I may not remember passwords or phone numbers, but I do remember one zip code: OH two ONE three FOUR! Send me to ZOOM!

Stays Soggy In Milk: The One About Breakfast Cereals.

Oats, corn, wheat, and sugar: The building blocks of any non-nutritious breakfast as a kid. It was always more about the FORM of the flakes, not the substance. Captain Crunch and King Vitamin were essentially the exact same cereal, but with different career paths. Quisp may have come from outer space, but Pebbles came straight out of prehistoric Earth. There was room in the pantry for all of them.

As hard as our parents tried to get us to make the switch to the vitamin-enhanced healthy cereals like Wheaties or Special K, we remained fiercely loyal to the cereal-shaped candy bars guaranteed to shred the roofs of our mouths. I'm looking at YOU, Captain! If we ever did give in and pour a bowl of Colon Blow, the first thing we did was drown it in sugar. Fortified cereals tasted like rust if you didn't.

There were also the stunt cereals, like the oversized Honeycombs and the original ASMR known as Rice Krispies. Cereals with additives, such as marshmallows and raisins, were also a hit, as long as we didn't try to separate the elements. Whoever came out with whole bags of marshmallows or entire boxes of Crunch Berries was a true genius.

Craft Stores: Suburban Head Shops With Floral Tape

After spending my entire childhood with a mother who never met a craft she didn't like, I now have Plaster of Paris, Fun Film, and Mod Podge running through my veins. Mom generally switched between different projects, starting with Plaster of Paris pendants and then moving on to decoupage artworks culled from magazines. She saved the best for last: molded chocolate candies. It was double-boiler heaven for her assistant.

One of her favorite crafts involve the formation of plastic film flowers, using a questionable product called Fun Film. Fun Film was a combination of nail polish and illicit hallucinogens, a cousin to airplane glue and Super Elastic Bubble Plastic. Mom formed each petal and leaf from floral wire, then combined them into flowers using green floral tape. The results were universally impressive, but the contact high was a reward all its own.

Mom usually donated all of her craft projects to the school as fundraisers, but she occasionally sold a few pieces to earn enough money for more supplies. The local craft store became her version of a head shop, checking to see if they were holding any Fun Film or could hook a sister up with some styrofoam. Personally, I thought they stepped on the Mod Podge, man.

Spock Watch, Fred Bread, and Elton John: Facts Left Off The Brochures

With as little context as possible, here are some fast facts left out of my hometown's Chamber of Commerce brochures. An economics teacher used to put study hall violators on Spock Watch. The offender became Spock, and he or she had to report to "Captain Kirk" if a dot in the corner moved. Football legend Larry Csonka's mother used to deliver the mail. We once tried to change our school colors to pink and black, and call ourselves the Stow High Good and Plenties.

Fred Bread was an unwashed gym shirt stored in an abandoned locker and fed bread and water for a year. A librarian once spent an entire morning tracking down "Elton John" for an overdue book. At a talent show, someone swallowed 10 live goldfish before anyone could tell him about the last-minute baby carrot switch. If a carousel horse usually parked outside a McDonald's went missing, they checked the high school's courtyard first.

You can lead a cow up 3 flights of stairs, but you can't lead it back down. Ask me how I know. There was no pool on the roof, but plenty of pool passes to sell. LeBron James destroyed one of our basketball hoops. Someone carjacked a garbage truck and went on a rampage. At least that one was captured on video.

FROZEN CUSTARD

Frozen Custard Stands: Where God Gets His Ice Cream

If there was a downside to living 300 yards from a legendary local frozen custard stand, I never found it. The owners of Stoddard's had three frozen custard machines custom built to churn twice as slow as the competition, which meant a lot more butterfat and a whole lot less air whipped into the mix. Three machines also meant three flavors, which were routinely chocolate, vanilla, and a Flavor of the Day. The flavor of the day was a true Mystery Date– it could be a dream (blueberry), or a dud (butter rum).

Until the Internet allowed the flavor of the day to be discoverable, part of the fun was the 300 yard dash from my house. The pace would change according to the contents of the sign. If it was banana or strawberry, it became a gallop. If it was a less enticing flavor, it was a saunter. I was always envious of the older neighborhood kids who got to work at the custard stand, because legend had it they were allowed to eat their mistakes. Did someone say "Oops"?

Because the factory responsible for God's ice cream burned down in 1949, those machines were babied beyond belief. I also have a deliberately dim memory about challenging ourselves to order the worst thing possible. Unless someone else orders a butterscotch slushy, I'm still claiming the title.

A Vision In Black and White: The Generic Food Craze

My childhood grocery store surprised us all by installing new food aisles in the late Seventies. Soon, the shelves were filled with a new concept in no-frills grocery shopping: generic food. Instead of Kool-Aid or Lay's, budget-conscious shoppers could now put "drink mix" or "potato chips" in their carts. The packaging went beyond minimalism. The containers were white, with simple black lettering. You wanted corn chips, you got "corn chips".

While the generic food craze had a boffo first act, with cans and bottles and boxes flying off the new shelves, the flaws in the "ointment" soon became apparent. To put it mildly, quality was Job 4. In order to maximize profit and minimize food cost, the powers-that-be running Generic Town simply found third-tier food manufacturers willing to produce a cookie-like product, sir. Generic tortilla chip bags contained corn chips over there, clumps of nacho cheese powder over there, and all the flavor you've come to expect from cardboard.

The generic food craze did not last long, fortunately. The novelty had worn off, and customers on a budget began investing in store brands and off-brands with slightly higher production values. I won't forget the brief, shining moment when generics were actually boss, however.

The Projector Sector: Fraternity, Equality, Visibility

One of the best days at school began when the TV cart entered the room, the shades were pulled, and the lights went off. This meant 29 out of 30 students would soon be enjoying an episode of Sesame Street, ZOOM, or The Electric Company. The other kid became a deputy of the audio-visual squad, otherwise known as the Projector Sector.

Due to the uncertainties of UHF reception, our only hope of cutting through the snow and static was a classmate and an indoor antenna. He would perform an intricate set of moves while perched on a desk not engineered for interpretive dance. The picture would fade in and out until the teacher determined a sweet spot. While the rest of us watched Mister Rogers toss his shoe, the Projector Sector volunteer bravely manned his post.

Whether it was waiting for the beep of a sputtering slideshow or dutifully wheeling an overhead projector from classroom to classroom, those of us on the audio-visual squad still have fond memories of serving both Man and Seventies technology.

Atomic Fireballs: The First Cryptocurrency

For those who believe that cryptocurrency includes names like Bitcoin, Doge, and Ethereum, allow me to introduce you to a cinnamon-flavored jawbreaker known as an Atomic Fireball. Atomic Fireballs could be purchased by the each or in bulk at all the discerning candy stores in my hometown. To the rest of the world, Atomic Fireballs may have been a pact between the Devil and the town dentist, but to us they were a vital part of the schoolyard shadow economy.

You could always trade Atomic Fireballs for other types of candy, trading cards, or even cinnamon toothpicks, the legal loophole around the "no gum in class" edict. There were no set exchange rates, just whatever the market would bear. Inevitably, a few Atomic Fireball robber barons with more indulgent parents or better candy store connections took over most of the action. I'm still into Big Chuck for twenty large.

Atomic Fireballs eventually lost their cache as more and more dealers became users, and we found other commodities to exchange. Wacky Packs, anyone?

HOMER
HUMER
DANUAR

We're Mad, We're Cracked, We're Wacky: Subversive Comic Books That Shaped Us

The year is 1970, and a young boy from the suburbs of Akron, Ohio discovers a comic book that would change his life forever. It was called Mad Magazine, and its snarky tone and sensory overload artwork left Richie Rich and Archie in the dust. Mad Magazine introduced pre-teen boys to R-rated movies and edgy song parodies and spies going against spies. The movie parody in this issue happened to be about "Patton", and it would be years before I could actually see the real thing.

After getting comfortable with Mad's stickers, fold-ins, and Don Martin's whatever that was, it was time to branch out. Mad's main competitor for the hearts of nerds was called Cracked. Cracked Magazine was a little less sophisticated than Mad. It didn't rely on subtleties or clever word play. Cracked understood its key demographic, and became the Mad magazine you got when mom wouldn't let you have the real deal.

The grocery store shelf cousin to both magazines was a series of trading cards called Wacky Packages, or Wacky Packs for those in the know. Wacky Packs used garish comic book imagery to mock real products, like A-Jerks Cleanser or Hungry Jerk pancake mix. Wacky Packs eventually buckled under the weight of trademark infringement, but it was fun while it lasted.

BOOKSTORE

The School Bookstore: A Janitor's Closet Filled With Wonders

The annual back-to-school trek to stores like K-Mart and Sears was supposed to meet all of our clothing, Trapper Keeper, pencil box, and crayon needs, but sometimes protractors and compasses just happen. Sometimes, erasers just fall off—the universe can be cruel that way.

For those first-grade world problems, there was a solution: the school bookstore. The school bookstore only existed for a few short minutes before classes started, so timing was everything. It was a converted janitor's closet, and was usually manned by the giants of the elementary school, sixth graders. Need a new eraser? Five cents, please. A little light on the wide ruled paper and fat pencils? Ten cents, please. It was a racket for sure, but the bookstore could still hook a brother up.

I actually got to work a shift or two at the bookstore, as a worldly sixth grader. With minimal on-the-job training, I managed to serve the public good with a positive attitude and the promise of a free lunch for my efforts. Not bad for a 15 minute gig.

Fruit Float, Fruit Float, Fruit Float: If Jello And Yogurt Had A Love Child.

In the world of food fads and trends, there are perennial favorites that disappear without warning, like Maple Nut Goodies, and food lab experiments that were born to die. Libby's Fruit Float was definitely in that second camp. Fruit Float was a concentrated slurry of a dairy product, sweetener, thickening agents, and real fruit pieces, typically strawberries, pineapples, and peaches.

Consumers would pour this starter pack into a large bowl and mix it with cold milk. This was where the magic happened. After a few minutes in the fridge, it would congeal into a creamy treat somewhere between Jello pudding and yogurt. Essentially, it tasted like what you HOPED yogurt would taste like, but didn't.

The promotion of Fruit Float consisted of commercials challenging people to say Fruit Float three times fast, which in my mind is not the best quality of a brand name. "I dare you to pronounce this stuff!" The product itself was only on store shelves for about a year or two before it disappeared without ceremony. There are many of us old-timers who would still like to watch it wiggle, and finally become The Blob in a bowl.

Merlin and the Bliptones: Kicking It Retro-School

In a world where Grand Theft Auto is no longer just a felony, it's hard to believe that children of the Seventies were highly entertained by a single electronic blip. We sent that blip flying across the TV screen in Pong. We fired blips at low-rez Space Invaders. Blips turned big Asteroids into little Asteroids. We even ran a blip across a "football field" until we heard the buzzy chirp of a victory march.

For the hipper-than-thou crowd with indulgent parents, there were home video consoles with names like Atari, Coleco, and Intellivision. For the rest of us, there was a local department store with those consoles positioned just out of reach on endcaps. We would take turns risking life and limb for a few precious moments of playtime. Inevitably, what started with Pac Man eventually became Blip Dude at Christmas.

One of the holy grails of electronic games was Merlin, a combination of Simon, Tic-Tac-Toe, and a Magic Ring puzzle. Merlin looked like something Spock would use to detect alien lifeforms, but it checked a lot of our entertainment boxes. If you had three hours to kill and the patience of a saint, you could actually program it to play Jingle Bells. It also reminded us how pointless Tic-Tac-Toe really was, but at least we didn't have to dangle from a store shelf just to play it.

Superballs: The Juicy Fruit of Seventies Toys

There's a reason why Superballs of old rarely became old Superballs. They performed their job TOO well.

It all started with a commercial demonstrating a revolutionary rubber ball forged under fifty thousand pounds of pressure at a mysterious toy factory. They even had a name for its life force: Zectron. Once a Superball started bouncing, whether under a table, down the stairs, or off the top of a building, it never stopped bouncing. In fact, it seemed to pick up steam.

Every rubber ball ever made before 1964 paled in comparison to the Superball. Using a Superball to play Jacks was completely out of the question. It only took a slight miscalculation for a Superball to break free and treat the entire room like Godzilla treated Tokyo.

The main reason most Superballs had the shelf life of Juicy Fruit gum was the overwhelming temptation to test them out from the highest point a ten-year-old could reach, usually a bedroom window or a garage. That trick worked once, and we all got to watch our Zectron-enhanced Superballs bounce down the driveway, never to be seen again.

Monster Chiller Horror Theater: The Supe's On In Cleveland

IN ORDER TO FILL THE air with reruns of Gilligan's Island or The Brady Bunch, local television stations in the Seventies had to make a package deal with the studio devils. They could get the rights to a few popular sitcoms or cartoons or Westerns, but they also had to accept thousands of Grade Z horror movies and obscure Hollywood titles as well. The stations usually showed the good shows when they knew kids would be watching, and held off on the schlock until after the late night news.

This is why many mild-mannered program directors like Marty Sullivan from WUAB in Cleveland would become hosts of ultra-low budget horror shows. Sullivan himself donned a set of pajamas emblazoned with an S, and became Superhost. If a movie featured wasp women or 50 foot tall men or radioactive bacteria, it found a home on his Saturday afternoon show.

The show's opening was pure Cleveland humor gold. In his haste to change into his Super Host costume, Marty drops a gold-plated Chuck Taylor tennis shoe. When an innocent bystander picks it up, he grabs it and yells "GIMME DAT SHOE!" Sigh, the price we paid for Hogan's Heroes and Yogi Bear.

The Fourth Grade Skillset Not On My Linked In Profile.

Ventriloquism. What was the thinking here? Much like algebra, I've never had to avoid moving my lips in a dark alley, but that didn't stop me from ordering the "how to throw your voice" pamphlet and learn how to replace half the alphabet with either D or T. My dummy didn't blink, turn its head, or deliver snappy punchlines. It moved its lips up and down, the one thing I wasn't allowed to do myself.

Walking on stilts. Riding a unicycle was a skill. Juggling was a skill. I envied those who could do both at the same time. Following a short learning curve, walking on stilts was just a matter of deciding to do it. Maybe one kid in a thousand got to try those circus stilts that shot up 20 feet in the air. The rest of us could only manage a two foot lift, until it became a 6 inch slog on soaking wet ground.

Magic. David Blaine performs magic. David Copperfield performs magic. The best a kid could do was not get in the way of a self-working gimmick. The real trick was finding what the professionals called "patter". As much stage fright as I had, it felt like I had finally combined ventriloquism with magic after all. No lips dared to move during my attempts at patter.

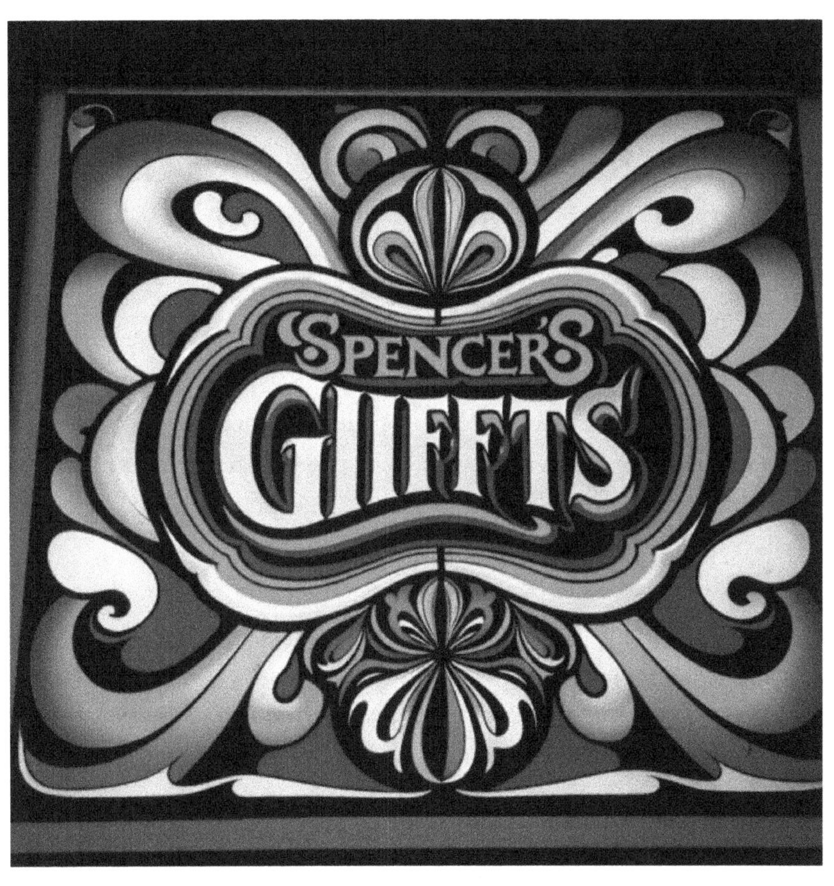
SPENCER'S
GIIFFTS

The Back Room Of Spencer's Gifts: Remember What The Dormouse Said

The local shopping mall in the 70s was the best place to find cookies, clothes, summer sausage kits, shoes, and weird orange drinks under one roof, but cool kids who knew what time it was headed straight for the alternative nation known as Spencer's Gifts. The front half of Spencer's played it straight, with gag gifts featuring rubber dog poo competing for shelf space with snarky coffee mugs and greeting cards for relatives with an actual sense of humor.

The back room of Spencer's was where suburban boys and girls first tasted the day-glow wild side. Harsh fluorescent lighting was replaced with a thing called "black light." Black light gave anything remotely white a radioactive sheen, and there were dozens of posters featuring forbidden fruits such as Grateful Dead artwork and Pink Floyd album covers. The unmistakable scent of patchouli incense wafted over us.

The sensory overload continued with strobe lights, plasma displays, and light organs that reacted to music. Lava lamps and black lights were a match made in hippie heaven. The trickiest part was to recover from this contact high before Mom whisked us off to the matinee movie. Star Wars, I KNOW what you're doing now, and I LIKE it.

Amaze Your Friends For Just Shipping And Handling

There's a reason why this country hasn't been overrun by 7-foot tall, life-like monsters, and it can be found in the back of old comic books. Once you get past the fake Utopia of Sea Monkeys (spoiler alert: brine shrimp) and quit trying to make smoke from your fingertips, the monsters and cardboard submarines took over. Your own personal Frankenstein was only a dollar thirty-five away from fruition.

The time between ordering your new friend and its arrival in your mailbox was the longest in recorded history. How is the mailman even supposed to get a seven foot tall monster out of the truck and into your room? Did it have enough to eat, and could it breathe? As it turned out, the whole "creature" managed to fit in one business-size envelope.

Truth in advertising is a movable feast, especially when it comes to ads in the back of comic books. My new life-like monster turned out to be a 7-foot long sheet of plastic, accompanied by a balloon with Frankenstein's face on it. Once folded like the Shroud of Turin, my 3 and a half foot buddy didn't exactly amaze any of my friends. MOM thought it was funny.

MERCUROHCROME

This May Sting A Little: The Lie That Was Mercurochrome

As most of us can attest, these knees were made for skinning, and that's just what they did. Open wounds and childhood were the default setting, from road rash to trips on the playground. The next step in the semi-healing process was always a memorable disinfection ritual with products Mom always seemed to have on ready-five status.

The first was Bactine, whose major selling point was its relatively pain-free nature. A little squirt of Bactine in the field was good enough for most incidents. The bump up for more serious abrasions was hydrogen peroxide, which might have stung a little bit, but the fascinating foaming action made up for it. It was just fun to watch.

Things took a definite turn for the worse when Mom produced a bottle of furniture stain/paint remover called Mercurochrome. Mercurochrome was mercifully removed from store shelves eventually, but when it was the king of disinfectants, the screams could be heard for miles. It didn't come to play, and many of us wore the orange tattoo as a badge of courage.

Blister Pack In The Sun: The Kid-Friendliest Toy Aisle Ever

Every self-respecting department store had a juvenile version of Mecca known as the toy section. The instant a family entered the store, the children set a new land speed record to get there. Most of the aisles featured brands such as Mattel, Hasbro, and Kenner, and price tags such as $14.95 and $29.95. This is where the phrases "maybe for your birthday" and "make sure you tell Santa" were born.

Meanwhile, there was an entire aisle in the toy section that gave children of all ages and tax brackets hope. Racks of toys protected by blister packs were hung by the endcaps with care, hoping parents with a little disposable income soon would be there. The blister pack toys included Whizzers, Jacks, Uno cards, and the ultimate childhood hallucinogen, Super Elastic Bubble Plastic.

The blister pack aisle rarely had recognizable brand names, and the price tags often read one dollar or less. We may not have been able to take home a Star Wars model or a Toss Across, but there was every chance we could leave the store with a yo-yo or a box of caps. If I had a hammer...

Going Bottomless

I believe all those who call themselves serious coffee drinkers should go bottomless as often as possible. While your neurons try desperately to erase that imagery, allow me to explain. Before this country became one giant parking lot for Starbucks, we had diners, roadside grills, greasy spoons, holes in the wall, mom-and-pop stands, donut shops, burger joints, and other examples of American gastronomic superiority. All of these establishments had one thing in common- the patented Bottomless Cup of Coffee. For a few measly quarters, one could enjoy an endless supply of industrial-strength motor oil coffee, refilled at critical moments by sympathetic hands.

Going bottomless is not for the faint of heart- it's a lifestyle choice that demands a lot of dedication from its practitioners. If you go bottomless, be prepared to have an opinion on everything, from national politics to what's wrong with these kids today. Bottomless coffee isn't served by 18 year old college freshmen named Brittany or Kelli- it's flung out by waitresses named Edna or Polly or Eunice. These angels in comfortable shoes have already been there, already done that, and have strapped on the apron to prove it. When you go bottomless long enough, the fourth wall between waitress and customer comes down with a satisfying thud.

The entire Bottomless Cup industry hinges on ritual. The first cup- only a warm-up swing, a little loosening of the pipes. The second cup comes around, and suddenly, the world is a much nicer place. Now is a great time to fling out the best thought on your mind- get it on the table and see who runs with it. By the time cup three rolls around, you notice that Edna looks a little tired. The debate over Ginger or Mary Ann is still raging strong, though, so now's not the time to pry. Cup four is usually the deal-breaker unless you have a hollow leg. Mary Ann is leading by a wide enough margin for you to make a dignified exit. You make your goodbyes, pat Edna platonically on the arm, and slip her an extra dollar for her troubles. Another Bottomless day is complete.

Now go out there and grab yourself a bottomless cup o' Joe, for old time's sake. Oh yeah- and tell Edna I sure do miss her cooking.

FIZZIES: LUKEWARM NECTAR OF THE CHILDHOOD GODS

The other night I asked a bartender to do something I would probably never ask a plastic surgeon or auto mechanic to do- just surprise me. She came back with a drink she called a Nutty Monk- part coffee, part Frangelico and part Irish Cream. I said to myself this has got to be the most adult beverage I've ever tasted. The hazelnut flavor of the Frangelico mixed perfectly with the dark coffee, and the Irish Cream mellowed it all out. Absolutely delicious, I must say.

But if a Nutty Monk was the most adult beverage I'd ever tasted, then what would be my choice for the best childhood beverage? I had the usual suspects (chocolate milk, Nehi sodas, Chillee Willees and milkshakes), but I finally settled on the perfect drink of my earliest childhood- Fizzies.

Fizzies were produced by the fine people who brought us Alka-Seltzer, and after a few Nutty Monks I have begun to appreciate the irony. Fizzies came in the standard cola flavors, like orange, grape, lemon-line and a sort of coca-cola, but my favorite was the root beer. All a kid had to do was plop, plop and wait patiently for the fizz, fizz to die down. Few of us ever waited, which left us with that indescribable feeling of half a seltzer tablet sliding down our gullets. But oh, the flavors that would just burst out of the glass. A day without Fizzies was like a day without sunshine, so we would make sure that mom included them on her shopping list. I can still taste the last Fizzie I ever had.

Alas, Fizzies met an ignoble fate at the hands of modern science. The only sweeteners capable of withstanding the mysterious Fizzie manufacturing process were cyclamates, which were banned from use in American products around 1969. The last Fizzie plopped unceremoniously into its last glass of tap water around 1971 or so. I would like to think of that time as the day the bubbles died. I have found other beverages to replace Fizzies in my glass, but I haven't really found one to replace Fizzies in my heart. Maybe someday I'll ask a bartender to surprise me again, and he'll hand me a Rootbeer Fizzie on the rocks.

So Whatever Happened to Saturday Morning Cartoons?

THIS SHOULD TEACH ME a little something about the pitfalls of nostalgia. I decided I would brew me up a nice pot of coffee, sit down in front of the tube and watch Saturday morning cartoons. EEEEEK! (ahem)

There was no Scooby Doo, no Bugs Bunny, no Laff-a-Lympics. Hell's bells, there wasn't even a Hong Kong Phooey. I found myself deeply mired in the muck and sludge that is Saturday morning cartoons today. I watched helplessly as anonymous bug-eyed heroines fought valiantly(?) against even more anonymous villains. Thankfully, I only had to endure about an hour of this onslaught until the networks decided I needed to watch sports or buy real estate at 10 am on a Saturday.

When I was a child, we were drawn to Saturday morning cartoons like hyperactive moths to a sugar-fed flame. We looked forward to seeing that genius Coyote set up his Rube Goldbergian house of cards in search of fresh Roadrunner meat. Apparently they just handed out genius cards to any old creature who wanted one, considering his abysmal success/failure rate. I actually remember keeping score during the Laff-a-Lympics, rooting for anyone who could wipe that smug grin off Snidely's face.

Now here's the plot to every cartoon on television: A band of cute Speed Racer look-alikes live in Harmonyville, USA. A heavily armored, gravel-voiced villain with anger management issues decides he wants to mess up their idyllic playground. The slowest of the good batch is either injured or captured by mindless henchmen. Only through teamwork and the aid of powerful laser technology can Cute triumph over lukewarm Evil, and said bad guy is promptly dispatched with extreme prejudice. Cute dolls sold separately, batteries not included.

I can understand that more mommies and daddies want to see news instead of Captain Kangaroo these days, but I sincerely hope cartoons make a glorious comeback in my lifetime. I've got serious money riding on the Coyote if they do.

Tenk You, Boyza

YOU DON'T HAVE TO BE Norwegian to understand Lawrence Welk, but apparently it helps. The other night I had my trusty mug of coffee in one hand and the tv remote in the other, scanning the channels man-style for something to watch. You know what man-style channel surfing is like- give each channel exactly three nanoseconds to prove itself worthy of a stop. Sad to say, partial nudity does play a part in the decision-making process.

I took a few sips of strong, dark courage and eventually settled on the red-headed stepchild of the free broadcast world- PBS. In defense of public television, may I say how fun it would be to watch a show like Fear Factor have to beg for every nickel it needs, while the Antiques Roadshow gets a million dollars per episode. But I digress.

There on my screen stands bandleader Lawrence Welk, fronting a band outfitted in what can only be described as early Paintshop Explosionwear. I understand that color television was a new and wondrous thing in Welk's day, but couldn't they have limited the clothing scheme to colors that exist in nature? I managed to catch some episodes from the early 60s, and I must say the boys looked mighty sharp in their tailored, thin-lapeled suits with the Cuban boots. Then all of a sudden the spirit of good taste and restraint passed right over the studio door. The result was a collision between a Day-Glo paint truck and a circus train.

Even more disconcerting than the clothes were the performers themselves. I had no idea you could actually airbrush a live human being. Maybe it was the coffee talking, but I started to feel like I had tripped into the Stepford Wives Comedy Variety Hour by mistake. All that was missing was a surprise appearance by the Pointer Sisters and the comedic stylings of Mr. David Brenner.

You know, it's a funny thing about nostalgia. Dylan might have been onto something when he said 'what looks large from a distance/ Close up ain't never that big', but when it comes to the Lawrence Welk show and all of its apparent corniness, perhaps it's we who have gotten smaller somehow. Enna one, enna two…

New Words For the Coffeehouse Generation

I'm always on the search for words that should exist but don't. The other day I tried out two new ones, wifittude and husbanality. Wifittude is what husbands receive when their chore list becomes an ignore list. Husbanality is a generic term for all those stories your spouse insists on retelling, under the mistaken belief that they are universally hilarious.

Here are some new words for the coffee house generation:

Slurgle: The first tentative sip of coffee you take before deciding if it's safe to swallow.

Janglicide: Unilateral decision that the only way to cure your caffeine shake is with more coffee.

Shotophobia: Irrational fear that your shot of hazelnut syrup will turn out to be bubblegum-flavored instead.

Grande Envy: Noticing the KFC-chicken-bucket-sized-cups everyone else seems to be ordering.

Javachum: Those irresistible candies and snacks which only seem to taste right with gourmet coffee.

Brevado Delirium: Ordering your coffee in the grand style of Niles Crane, only to end up with a cup of hot water and an oreo cookie.

Mochavision: The perceived ability to see through walls after five shots of espresso.

Brewfluvia: The pile of empty sugar packets, candy wrappers, coffee cups and napkins left by the previous occupants of your prized corner table.

Browzilla: Bookstore code for a patron who skims through every best-seller while nursing a 50 cent cup of coffee.

"Jaux Pas": Any mistake made while ordering which results in suppressed laughter from the staff.

The Revolution WILL Be Televised, Right After The Midnight Special

Most Stowbilly children, especially teenagers, knew that the really good stuff didn't show up on TV until at least 11:30 on a Friday night. That's when Channel 8 in Cleveland handed over the reins to a weatherman and a broadcast engineer, AKA Hoolihan and Big Chuck. Hoolihan and Big Chuck's show was an amalgamation of schlocky horror movies, song parodies, Certain Ethnic jokes and sketch comedy clearly filmed on the cheap with someone else's equipment. It was pure camp, but we watched every last minute of it, all the way to the last segment where Hoolihan and Big Chuck, dressed in tacky animal print pajamas, would read jokes submitted by their loyal viewers. We needed to hear these jokes, because we would inevitably be retelling them at school on Monday morning. By the end of the broadcast, we would be too exhausted to move from the couch to the TV set, so we just let it run. We...just...let...it...run.

The end of Hoolihan and Big Chuck may have signaled the final gasp of local programming, but it was not the end of late night television as we knew it. Our sleep-deprived Midwestern minds could still be blown by the rock concerts featured on another channel. It may have been Don Kirschner's Rock Concert or The Midnight Special, like any of us could tell the difference at 1 in the morning. Whichever show it was, Cousin It and the Cousin It Band were usually getting down with their bad selves on a smoke-filled stage. All I remember is that they were scary to watch, but clearly devoted to their craft. They may have been the Allman Brothers, they may have been Blue Oyster Cult, they may have even been the Doobie Brothers or Foghat, but whatever it was, it was clearly a taste of music from the land of cool people. It's just too bad we weren't nearly awake enough to let sonic art wash over us.

For those of us whose parents did not believe in the beauty of cable television, another late night music show became our own version of MTV. NBC would show two hours of last year's hottest videos, but we didn't care. We got to see Adam Ant and Cyndi Lauper and Talking Heads and...well, those other guys with the hair. I think they had synthesizers, but don't quote me on that. While The Midnight Special and Rock Concert may have an abundance of soul, the late night video show on NBC had the promise of a Madonna-like product, sir. Life for a bleary-eyed Stowbilly boy became much better as soon as he learned a Go-Go or Bangle or Benatar would play a significant role in it. With the arrival of home VCRs, the late night music video show became one of the first things we learned to program on the timer.

Meanwhile, the comedy was still going strong on other channels, even if it took a turn to the left. If Saturday Night Live was the best American late night sketch comedy of its day, then SCTV was its hipper Canadian cousin. The cast of SCTV read like a Who's Who of comedy, from John Candy to Rick Moranis to Eugene Levy, with stops in-between for Martin Short, Andrea Martin, Joe Flaherty and Catherine O'Hara. SCTV, which stood for Second City Television, had the luxury of taping their segments over time, but they still maintained a sense of immediacy like Saturday Night Live. Characters like Doug and Bob McKenzie, horror show host Count Floyd and the Five Neat Guys became the stuff of legend. If another kid at school quoted the Farm Film Report ("he blowed up. He blowed up REAL good), then you knew he was hip to the same late night jive. It was one thing to stay up until the pajama jokes on Hoolihan and Big Chuck, but something else entirely if you stayed up until the end credits of SCTV. There were many Sunday mornings when devoted SCTVers would drag themselves to church or simply call in sick and sleep until noon.

In Space, No One Can Hear Spock Scream

As I pour a fresh pot of coffee down my thermos, I'm reminded of all those thermoses (thermi?) which have come before.

I honestly couldn't say what the very first beverage I ever drank out of a thermos was, but my gut says Kool-Aid. I distinctly remember picking out an Aladdin Partridge Family lunchbox on that inevitable Back to School trek to our local K-Mart. I came ever so close to the outdated Star Trek model, but uncooler heads prevailed. Inside this seemingly indestructible casing was a matching thermos, complete with full-length drawings of Susan Dey, my future wife. I'd never seen a thermos up close before- it was still one of those Space Age deals. I eagerly screwed off the lid... the cup... the lid AND the cup. Darn, those astronauts are clever.

A brand new thermos has one of those distinctive smells, like a new car or grandma's bathroom. I looked at the shiny aluminized innards for a good long while. This thermos and I would share beautiful moments together- a steady companion in the uncertain world of second grade. As long as Lori Partridge was within my grasp, nothing could go wrong.

About twenty minutes later, something went horribly wrong. I grabbed a marble from the floor and casually dropped it down the gullet of my new thermos. In a moment worthy of the second choice Star Trek lunchbox crew, all heck broke loose. The sides of the thermos lining shattered, followed by a sudden explosion as the hull was breached and the vacuum of space claimed the remains. My Susan was a shattered collection of glass shards and broken dreams. The trip back to K-Mart was deafeningly silent. The store was completely sold out of

Partridge Family thermoses, so I had to settle for what remained on the shelves.

Anyone know if a 1972 vintage Holly Hobby thermos is worth anything?

SO WHAT HAVE YOU BEEN DOING?

As I take a few reflective sips of coffee this morning, I'm reminded of an impending personal milestone. For reasons which will soon become apparent, I'm tempted to change that to read 'personal MILLstone'.

Next year will mark my twentieth season out of high school. Of course you realize this means plane tickets, ill-fitting suits, complete memory loss, hotel reservations and an open bar. Guess which one will get my fullest attention. It's not that I'm against the need for class reunions on some intellectual plane, but sometimes I question the wholesale marketing of what may be a rather painful yardstick for some. I anticipate receiving quite a few unsolicited invitations from companies who specialize in class reunions. I have a feeling I'm going to separating a little wheat from a boatload of chaff when January arrives.

At first I feared that no one from my class would even find me. I just knew I'd end up on that collective Wanted Poster you always see in the local newspaper. Now with the glories of the Internet in full bloom, my new fear is that EVERYONE will find me. I can't speak for all of you, but don't you sometimes think of your former classmates as perpetual teenagers? My last contact with 90% of my class was in the years of Reaganomics and fluorescent clothing. I'm not sure I'm ready to meet the modern editions who will show up en masse at the one country club in my hometown. I just know I'm going to expect parachute pants and leg warmers a-plenty, while the DJ plays Duran Duran and a Flock of Seagulls.

As badly as I want to meet the accountants, teachers, housewives and small business owners of today, part of me still wants to crawl back into the 80s womb and talk about Luke and Laura's wedding all night. Nostalgia isn't everything, but sometimes it's the thing that will keep you the warmest.

THE GREAT HYMNAL WAR

As I drink my coffee this morning, I think about my pseudo-career in music. I have always been interested in music, ever since I taught myself to play one of those wheezy Magnus chord organs when I was 4. The Magnus people made learning a breeze with their idiosyncratic numbering system. I still enjoy playing 5-6-5-3-5-6-5-3, and that beautiful love ballad 1-4-3-5-3-5. Eventually, I took up the clarinet and learned a little something about music theory. Little did I know how much of an impact this early musical education would have on my life.

When I was 12, we joined the pew-jumping, chandelier-swinging church next door to our house. In reality it was an Apostolic Pentecostal church, but you know how rumors get started. The pastor was a firm believer in the encouragement of 'young people', which surely included me at the time. His wife was the church pianist, a young associate pastor was the organist, a family of country singers played guitars and yours truly became the accordionist. My Magnus chord organ skills paid off in spades as I dutifully plowed through any song mentioning the Blood of the Lamb. One thing about Pentecostal music- the Blood had better be flowing, or else we're not playing it. For the four years I played in that orchestra, I was steeped in foot-stomping, hand-clapping good old gospel music.

Twenty-some-odd years later I find myself being asked to play the organ for a small country Methodist church in Alabama. Full of my former Pentecostal vim and vigor, I eagerly agreed to take on the challenge. Oh ye of little research. I found myself deeply embroiled in what can only be called the Great Hymnal War. The old hymnals could conceivably be divided into dirge/not dirge, while the absolute newest versions might as well have included 'Jesus is just alright with me'. Somewhere in the middle was the accepted hymnal, which incorporated just enough of both camps to be perfectly contentious to musicians. I'm actually enjoying the schizophrenia, as I quietly plug away on a real church organ every Sunday. But every once in a while, I find myself wanting to strap on an old accordion and see how strong those ceiling joists really are.

THERE'S MUSIC IN THAT THERE COFFEE, MISTER.

As I settle down to my final cup of coffee for the day, I hear the opening strains of Van Morrison's "Brown-Eyed-Girl" and realize how good life can get. I'm not sure what the most perfect song in the world would sound like, but I think John Prine is going to write it and Van Morrison is going to sing it. If they don't, I'm sure Tom Waits, Bruce Springsteen or Bob Dylan will be on ready five status.

Surprisingly enough, coffee shows up in a lot of memorable songs. Mickey Dolenz promises time for "coffee-flavored kisses and a bit of conversation" in the Monkee's *Last Train to Clarksville*. Don Williams begins his lonesome day with "coffee black, cigarette" in his country hit *Some Broken Hearts Never Mend*. Bob Dylan lingers over *One More Cup of Coffee* before facing (*The Valley Below*).

Oddly enough, I don't believe the Beatles ever mentioned coffee in their music, but one might wonder what was in the cup Paul speaks of in *A Day in the Life*.

Coffee is almost always the one bit of normalcy that creeps into the songwriter's otherwise complicated verses. We can all identify with that desperate search for the waitress, or that early morning jolt of reality only coffee can bring.

For a long time, I thought Van Morrison's *Into the Mystic* was as close to perfection as anyone could get. Now I'm beginning to think that we are all responsible for writing our own perfect song, one where the verses don't really matter and all our friends know the chorus by heart.

YOU KNOW THAT WE ARE LIVING IN A COFFEE WORLD

My wife tells me that she's been drinking coffee since she was four years old, and somehow I believe her. It may be the dozen or so cans of Story House gourmet coffee strewn around the house, or it may be the fact that we are already on our third coffeemaker in six years of marriage. We can't leave the local coffeeshop/bookstore without gazing longingly at the top-end cappucino machines and French press carafes on the shelves. You know those oversized bins of whole bean coffee at the grocery store? I'm beginning to think they're actually free gumball machines for coffee fanatics.

My wife says she started her coffee habit by finishing off the dregs of coffee left behind by her parents. My brother started drinking coffee at our mother's funeral. He started off with equal proportions of cream, sugar and coffee, then eventually acquired a taste for the stronger stuff. Being an inveterate hot tea drinker from way back, I still prefer a little cream and sugar in mine. My first real exposure to coffee was not in a cup, but one of those chewy coffee-flavored candies. I took one bite, expecting chocolate, and received a rather abrupt introduction to the world of coffee.

Some say the world is divided into two groups- those who like Neil Diamond and those who don't. I say that the world can be divided in a different way- the world we knew before coffee, and the one we discovered after that first cup. 'Coffee World' is inherently different- life has a few more edges, a little more color. Like any other first experience, you can sense that an invisible border has been irreversibly crossed, but somehow you don't seem to mind the change. Coffee World can be a challenging place sometimes, but its also worth trying all the way to the dregs.

WHAT'S NEXT—COFFEE-FLAVORED COFFEE?

I've been on a diet for about 6 months now, which explains why I just finished eating a bowl of coffee almond ice cream. Let he who is without carb cravings cast the first Slimfast can. Speaking of diet drinks, I believe more than a few companies have composed coffee-flavored variations on their standard liquid fare. Oh they try to be so clever by calling it 'mocha', but we see through their little ruse.

Over the years, there have been many attempts to blend coffee with another food or beverage. Some have proven hugely successful, while others have fallen a little short of the glory. Coffee ice cream came straight out of the vat with a halo and a large bow saying 'Buy me, I'm terrific!', while the earliest versions of cold cappucinos played cards on the shelves and said 'When you run out of every other drink in the house, you know where I live.' Times have changed, and now frozen or chilled cappucinos are among the most popular drinks in gourmet coffeehouses. Sometimes it just comes down to building the perfect beast and waiting for the right consumers to find it.

As appealing as it sounds, there is one coffee-enhanced beverage I'm glad hasn't made it onto store shelves-Drew Carey's infamous Buzz Beer. For those of you who missed the show, Buzz Beer came about after one of Drew's cronies started drinking coffee between taste tests. The combination proved to be marketable on the show, but I seriously doubt anyone would actually try to duplicate it in real life. Coffee has been used in a lot of strange concoctions, but beer seems to do best on its own. (At least I won't be polishing off a pint of beer pistachio ice cream any time soon). That's okay, though- it leaves more room in the fridge for my card-playing iced cappucino buddies.

THERE'S A DAY FOR THAT

I happen to be the proud owner of the most oxymoronic job title in the world- a professional poet. Historically, this has proven to mean I'll be long gone before the check for the pizza arrives. We poets live for April, which happens to be National Poetry Month. For a solid thirty days, poetry and poets can roam freely in the streets, without calling their parole officers or violating restraining orders.

April also happens to be National Coffee Month, which makes some sort of symbiotic sense to me. Coffeehouses were generally the first venues to embrace poets, so I can see sharing a month with the hands that feed us. All this talk about national months got me to thinking, though. You have to figure that for every month that makes sense (Black History Month, AIDS Awareness Month, Women in Sports Month, etc.) there must be hundreds that are best described as answers to obscure trivia questions. Creating a new 'Month' must be the bread-and-butter of legislators everywhere. It's got to be the best win/win situation of all time- instant respect for the lawmakers, and recognition of the oft-ignored blue-backed iguana owners of America.

I'd like to know who decides what cause deserves a national Day, Week, Month or Year. The negotiations have got to be the most delicate diplomatic operations in Washington DC: 'You know, Bill, I share your love for the little critters myself, but how about National Wombat DAY? We had to give Senator Jones "National Pantyhose Month", so the calendar's looking a little full right now.' No matter what the occasion, I'd like to think someone is waiting for the Wombat Parade of Heroes to pass by on that special day.

All I know is that next April, I will be sipping my gourmet coffee and working on my next collection of poems. If you care to join me, just remember I like extra pepperoni.

COFFEE NIPS: A GATEWAY CANDY?

I realized the other day that my first taste of coffee didn't come from a cup, but from a little piece of penny candy called a Coffee Nip. My dad used to take us to an indoor flea market on Saturdays, and one of the booths featured nothing but candy of every description. If we had a quarter or two, we could easily recreate the average Halloween haul. I fell hard for a piece of German-style chocolate called an Ice Cube. It wasn't like your average Chunky or Hershey Bar- it was incredibly smooth and creamy with a strong hazelnut flavor. At three cents a pop, it was the Cadillac of penny candies but I couldn't get enough of them. Our first and only goal on Saturdays was to seek out the 'Candy Lady' and load up our small brown paper bags.

On other days, we would ride our bikes up to a store called Reinker's, which was owned and operated by a sweet old German man. Mr. Reinker ran his store old-school style, with clerks that always knew your name and the best ice cream section in town. He would always insist on patting us on the head, which would simply offend our four year old sensibilities.

As I grew older, I discovered that Mr. Reinker also stocked an incredible assortment of penny, nickel and dime candies. Just behind the cashier stood the Wall of Paradise, complete with Ice Cubes and Coffee Nips.

But it didn't stop there, no sir. Reinker's carried the Holy Grail of collectibles for an eight year old kid- Wacky Packs. These were cards featuring spoofs of well-known products, like Dunder Bread and A-Jerks Cleanser. Each pack contained the ubiquitous stick of cardboard bubble gum, at least 5 stickers and a piece of a much larger puzzle. It was a glorious day when I actually had enough pieces to finish the mother of all things Wacky- the big puzzle.

I did some checking around the other day and found a supply of Ice Cubes online. They now go for thirty cents a piece. The Wacky Pack manufacturers cranked out their last run sometime in the late 80s or early 90s. The stickers I wasted as a child are now worth a fortune to serious collectors. I could be very sad about these twists of fate, but I'd much rather get another pat on the head from Mr. Reinker as he casually slips another Ice Cube into my mother's purse.

WOODLAND ELEMENTARY SCHOOL: PLAYGROUND CONFIDENTIAL

Woodland Elementary School came with its own proving ground, although outsiders often wrote it off as nothing more than a simple PLAYground. Those of us who ran through that unforgiving and cruel jungle know better. The playground at Woodland was actually a bit schizophrenic. There were sections designated as safe for grades K-3, then other areas deemed suitable. for the more discerning 4th to 6th grade crowd. This 38th parallel was never actually marked with a physical line on the asphalt or anything, but the younger kids instinctively knew when they were getting perilously close to crossing over it. It was Stow's version of a prison shock collar, only without the explosive charges. The K-3 crowd had to content themselves with games like hopscotch, which was barely a game in the first place, and the dreaded *small* swings. The teeter-totters were also divided between amateur and professional grade, although the one "game" that became universal was the sudden jump from the lower position, allowing gravity to take care of the victim in the higher position.

One popular playground game evolved from the innocent version we all played in the school's so-called multipurpose room. For a while, it was the gym for indoor PE classes, then it morphed into the lunchroom for meals, then became a gym again until the artistic urge took over and it became the auditorium for school talent shows or outside performances or whatever. While it was still a gym, however, we played the game known as dodge ball. Dodge ball was the straightforward version—there's a ball, dodge it. There was a natural upper limit to how much pepper could be put on those odd rubber balls only sold to schools, apparently. Throw, dodge, retrieve, throw again, hit, leave. These were all graspable concepts to a 4th grader.

Somewhere along the way, dodgeball became fireball. Fireball was similar to dodgeball only in the sense that fast-pitch baseball was similar to slow-pitch softball. Fireball was serious business, played by serious people. I remember one guy at Kimpton Middle School who could pick off any target of his choosing from across the entire gym floor. You could try to catch the ball, you could try to get out of the way, you could try to feign injury and leave, but Mark was eventually going to nail you with that fireball. Death by round rubber was in the cards. Once Mark got through picking off most of the opposing team, one unfortunate survivor who spent the entire game hiding behind others would be the last one standing. The PE teacher would declare a free fire zone, meaning no more lines were standing between competitors. Mark would stalk his prey for a few minutes, then deliver a crushing blow from three feet away. I think we ended up giving Mark both ears and the tail one time.

There was another game which was actually banned by the principal during my time at Woodland. Many of us can still remember the last words we heard before our collective lights went out: "Red Rover, Red Rover, let Mikey come over!". Red Rover was definitely a team sport, with two lines of players facing each other from a distance. The idea was to link arms and form an impenetrable human chain. A captain would select a challenger from the other side and lead his or her team in the taunting chant "Red Rover, Red Rover, let (insert name here) come over!". With that simple request, Inserted Name would try to break through the chain by any means necessary. If he or she was successful, a player would be sent back to the other side. If he or she could not break through, they became the newest link in that chain. This process of brute force elimination could stretch on for a while, I remember.

The Red Rover rot set in after more than a few Insert Names Here came on over as requested and failed miserably. Either they got clotheslined by the strongest links, or they inadvertently took out a few links of their own during an open field tackle situation. The Red Rover victim-to-champion ratio became far too lopsided for the prinicpal's liking, so he sent out a general bulletin that our Red Rover playing days were over. I remember a few people were sorely disappointed that their best head-butting days were now behind them, but it was a banner day for Insert Names Here everywhere.

One afternoon at Woodland, I watched two of our janitors drill a hole in the playground blacktop. They installed a tall aluminum pole and anchored it into the ground with cement. One of the janitors attached a long string to a hook at the very top of the pole, then attached what appeared to be a volleyball to the other end of the string.

Without much fanfare, the internationally ignored sport of tetherball had come to Stow. None of us knew exactly how the game was supposed to be played, but eventually the PE teacher did take us outside and explained the basic rules of tetherball. At long last, here was a game that made as little sense as possible and we actually stood in line waiting to play it. The best part was that helpless feeling at the very end as you watched your opponent wrap that ball around the pole at lightning speed.

One version of tetherball started out as a straight punch service, with the goal being to get past the other player and wrap the entire cord around the pole in a certain direction. This could be done through brute force or finesse, depending on the player's anger management skills. The other version called for the ball to swing slowly around the pole a few times in one player's direction, and then players could pounce on the ball at will. This was the version of tetherball that confused me the most. What other game on Earth started with one team watching helplessly as the other team loaded most of the bases? That three-turn advantage was devilishly hard to overcome, yet we would dutifully watch the ball wind around the pole like lemmings until that third spin. Tetherball was clearly a game sold to school administrators, not to the kids.

One "game" unique to Woodland was not really a game at all, but more of a dare. The back of the school's designated playground extended into a small woods. In order to keep students from wandering too far into those woods, rings were painted on several trees to serve as borders. The woods on one side of those border trees looked pretty much like the woods on the other side, but rules were rules. We were NOT to travel beyond those ringed trees, ever ever ever. Of course, there was no faster way to get some of us to disobey a school rule than by telling us not to do it.

By the time I was in 5th grade, the mythology of the Land Beyond The Painted Trees had become huge. There were stories of evil men who kidnapped trespassing children, who were of course never seen again. That was a good one for me—I would sometimes even stand guard near the ringed trees and look for anyone even a little suspicious. There were also tales of bears or coyote packs hiding in those woods, just waiting for free kids meals. Perhaps the best deterrents were all of those apocryphal stories about the punishment that awaited anyone who was caught behind those trees. In the unspoken Woodland criminal codes, crossing over into the Forbidden Zone during school hours was at the top of the list. I knew a few people who paid dearly for that brief taste of life outside the compound. I found out later, however, that there was a nice little trail that ran through those woods, and it ended at one of the least scariest places in Stow—the Stow-Kent Shopping Center. The school system spent years scaring us away from Kresge's department store and the A&P.

KIMPTON MIDDLE SCHOOL: Shh, I'm in the IRC becoming self-actualized.

From kindergarten until 6th grade, most of us Stowites attended the same elementary schools. We knew those places like the backs of our hands, and life during school time was mostly a matter of jumping through the hoops until the buses arrived. However, 7th grade was a completely different matter, and one that introduced apprehension to the curriculum. All of us who had previously identified as Woodlanders or Fishcreekers or Indian Trailers or whatever were now headed towards the One Middle School To Rule Over All, otherwise known as Kimpton. Preparing to go to Kimpton Middle School was the first inkling that recess as we knew it was indeed over.

Like a lot of other middle schools of its time, Kimpton subdivided its 7th and 8th grade students into instructional "teams". For students, this meant that we would be taught most of our subjects by the same four or five teachers assigned to our team. The team streams would rarely be crossed. I may have spent seven long years at

Woodland with a guy on team 7-1, but from this point on I was a member of team 7-2, and who knows what sort of shocking Pagan rituals those 7-1 types performed on warm weekend nights? I had my own suspicions on how these teams were selected, but nothing I could actually prove at the time.

Kimpton was much larger than the narrow halls of Woodland, and its immenseness was not lost on a small potato like me. We would all congregate in the cafeteria area just before classes began, and the first few weeks were usually spent looking for anyone anywhere who used to attend the same elementary school we did. But that summer between 6th and 7th grade seemed to have an effect on many of us. Yes, I did go to that much smaller elementary school in an entirely different city with that guy over there, but that's where the similarities now ended. We were all Kimptonites now, a young adolescent example of *e pluribus, unum*. It was now all about the *team*. What *team* are you on? Who's on OUR team? I hope *that* kid isn't on MY team. Kimpton was the opening two years of the 2-2-2 educational top or bottom, bottom or top schizophrenia that defined Stow's philosophy on higher learning for decades.

Speaking of educational philosophy, one of my teachers at Kimpton explained the underlying concept behind the apparent madness of the team teaching system. Kimpton was built at a time when a behavioral psychologist named Maslow was the man of the hour. Maslow, unlike his draconian predecessor Benjamin Skinner, believed that students (like all of God's children) learned best when their basic human needs were met. Maslow developed a triangular chart that listed the "Hierarchy of Needs", from the concrete items such as food, water and shelter to those more esoteric needs such as peace, love and understanding. Maslow was obviously a pinko and a hippie, but I digress. Once a person had all of these needs met, which could take an hour or a lifetime, then he or she would enter a Nirvana-like state called "self-actualization". A self-actualized middle school student was a happy middle school student, and much less likely to become a burden on local taxpayers years later.

In order to follow the path, excuse me, Path of self-actualization, a student at Kimpton should have felt free to explore his or her outside environment without getting so hung up on society's rules, man. In reality, we still needed hall passes to meet a few basic human needs Maslow conveniently left off the chart. We didn't go to the Establishment's "library", with its buzz-killing due dates and repressive Dewey Decimal system. Instead, we went to the IRC, the Instructional Resource Center. The IRC may have had the trappings of the Man's library, but we were free to explore our literary space at our own pace, and we liked it that way.

The cafeteria at Kimpton almost toppled this apple cart of harmonic self-actualization, however. French fries had long been a love/hate thing among students, since the elementary school offerings were usually thick frozen crinkle cut fries barely put through the deep frying process. At Kimpton, however, the cafeteria began to serve thinner shoestring french fries which came ever so close to duplicating the mythical McDonald's fries. The lunch ladies originally served these fries in huge cups, easily double the size of anything served elsewhere. A ritual for eating these fries soon formed. First, the cup would be overturned onto the serving tray. Salt would be added, accompanied by several small paper cups filled with ketchup. This mountain of potatoey goodness would be consumed quickly, lest the small problem of congealing oil spoil the process. That's how it worked for a few weeks, anyway.

As if straight out of a low-budget prison film, however, the polar opposite of self-actualization crept in. The fries became so popular so fast that others who missed out on them the first time would resort to stealing. Swiping someone else's fries became so commonplace that a lot of us would hold a metal fork in one hand while eating our fries with the other. Any inmate who tried to steal our fries ran a serious risk of getting the back of his hand aerated for free. Several students did in fact get stabbed, so the school took measures to curb their criminal impulses. Without admitting any tactical error on its part, the school switched out the metal forks for plastic ones. The stabbings could still take place, but the victory was largely academic. The cafeteria also switched to smaller cups, so the former excesses were no longer a factor.

Another idea borrowed from the Swinging Sixties was the belief that today's dabbler will become tomorrow's customer. Seventh graders were allowed to explore each and every creative or industrial art program for precisely six weeks at a time. This was usually enough time to decide if third degree burns from a spot welder were more to your liking than making (and compelled to eat) cookies made with four TABLESPOONS of baking soda. Students could also decide between a lack of native ability in visual art and a lack of native ability in music. During the eighth grade, enlightened students could choose two of these disciplines for a semester each. After learning how to sew an apron, make a wooden toaster tong, weld coiled wire into a trivet and make a sauce from orange juice and sugar, I opted for the music classes.

One of my music instructors was also a very talented folksinger and guitarist, although local venues were few and far between. We learned the basics of music composition, from scales to notation to rhythm, but I could tell his sweater vest-laden spirit was elsewhere. Every so often, he would break out his acoustic guitar and entertain the class with a passionate rendition of Harry Chapin's ode to absent parenting, "Cat's in the Cradle." He seemed especially wistful during the final verse, in which the son exacts karmic revenge on the inadvertently neglectful narrator/father. I can very easily imagine a major motion picture about his life: "Mr. R's Meaningful Folk Guitar with Hushed, Intimate Vocals Opus."

The other music instructor had a habit of standing in the hallway between classes holding a ukelele and a kazoo. As the young Van Halen and Led Zeppelin fans filed past his classroom door, he would blissfully saw away at a vintage Rudy Vallee or Al Jolson snippet for his own entertainment. Heaven knows WE weren't getting the job done. During class he would throw out challenges to the more musically inclined. One time he asked us all to sing a note as long as we could in a single breath. I remember it came down to me and my church friend and fellow musician Steve S. Steve and I looked at each other as the other competitors dropped out one by one. By the time it was over, Steve and I both looked like the poor opera singer tormented by Bugs Bunny inside the Hollywood Bowl.

Kimpton also provided an intramural sports program for any team members willing to sacrifice a lunch period for the sake of competition. Volleyball was a popular option, followed closely by basketball or dodgeball. The crowd-pleasing event, however, was tug-of-war. Almost all of us signed up for at least one session of tug-of-war, especially if it pitted class teams against each other. The rules were fairly straightforward: pull the rope until a centered flag crossed over a designated line. How any team accomplished that goal was strictly up to them. One popular but quasi-legal tactic was to creep forward on the rope whenever any gains were made. This would inevitably lead to one team controlling 99.5 percent of the total rope surface, while 20 other kids desperately held onto the remaining six inches. The other winning strategy was better known as Dean. Dean was one of the biggest guys in our class, and more than willing to share his talent with the rest of the players on his team. The new strategy involve tying one end of the rope around Dean's waist and keeping one hand on the rope for appearance's sake. The tug-of-war intramural battle was clearly for second place during the Dean years.

The two years spent in the welcoming and nuturing arms of educational visionaries like Maslow didn't exactly prepare 8th graders for the next step of the journey. All of us self-actualized little people were about to meet the AntiMaslow, a man named Skinner, in the rat maze and cheese collection known as Workman High School. But that's a story for another day.

WORKMAN HIGH SCHOOL:
Nothing a Ramp and Skinner Can't Handle

Practically every major building within the city limits of Stow served some other purpose at some other time in history. The building I knew as Workman High School, the one that serviced primarily 9th and 10th grade students, was at one time Stow High School, the only 9th-12th grade game in town. As Stow's population grew, the original building became hopelessly outgunned by the incoming student bodies. As many of us Stowbillies fondly remember, the city's solution to the problem was to find the best and the brightest architects it could afford, and these skilled men would come up with a solid plan to double the capacity of Stow High School. This scheme would have worked, too, if it hadn't been for those meddling measurements. The new addition was precisely one half-floor higher than the original building. Sorry about that, chief. Missed it by *that* much.

The marriage between old and new sections of Workman was finally achieved with a long, sloping ramp down the middle of a connecting hallway. Few of us missed any opportunity to slide or roll something down that ramp back in the day. The new section also had an elevator, although permission to use said elevator was limited to handicapped students or those who were temporarily out of commission. The rest of us had to choreograph an intricate ballet involving ramps, stairwells, hallways and more hallways. Workman's floor plan was dictated by the educational philosophy championed by Dr. Benjamin Skinner, a leading specialist in draconian teaching methods at the time. Dr. Skinner believed all a student really needed to learn was a desk and a teacher. Like rats in a maze, each student would eventually figure out the optimum way to travel from classroom to classroom. The reward for all of this behavioral conditioning was a quality education with minimal distractions. I would have preferred a lump of cheese myself.

The original part of Workman still featured steam-fed radiators for heat and open windows for non-heat. There was no air conditioning for the comfort of the rat students or their rat instructors. Dr. Skinner would have loved what they did with the place. During the colder months, the steam heat would flow through the cold metal pipes, causing them to expand and contract. This expansion and contraction triggered a series of loud bangs that could be heard throughout the building. It became our two minute warning that heat was finally on the way, one hallway at a time. The new part of Workman also had steam heat, but the architects were clever enough to hide the pipes under more modern covers. We could actually twist knobs that looked like they would have some effect on something. They didn't. Welcome to Ramp World.

One hallway in the original section led to the typing room, where many of us learned how to type on manual typewriters. The instructor would put on a record, and a man who sounded suspiciously like the narrator of every school filmstrip ever would call out letters to type. As we tapped our way through the "A...S...D...F...J...K...L...Sem" assignment over and over again, we had plenty of time to think of the things we'd rather be doing, like not typing endless lines of asdfjkl;. I always thought a sentence like "All work and no play makes Jack a dull boy." would be more interesting, just to see the look on the janitor's face when he emptied out trashcans from The Shining.

Our typing teacher at Workman did find ways to break up the homerow monotony, especially on Friday mornings. She allowed students to bring in their own albums while the rest of us sawed away at assignments printed in a workbook. I'm not sure if she was aware of the artistic leanings of the modern music scene at the time, but she wanted to be hip to the jive and we weren't about to stop her. Because we were so isolated from the rest of the building, volume was not an issue. So those of us who took certain typing courses under a certain typing/English teacher during the early 80s all learned to type while listening to AC/DC's heavy metal album "Back in Black". To this day, I can still hear the clacking of typewriter keys timed to the beat of the title song or "You Shook Me All Night Long".

The library at Workman was not especially spacious, but it was clearly a library, not a Kimptonian instructional resource center. The head librarian was one of those school employees you just knew had been there since brick one of construction. We called her the Mole Lady behind her back, but as deaf as she was, I'm sure we could have bypassed the pretense altogether. The standard procedure for checking out a book from the Workman library was to fill out a card with the student's name and hand it over to the librarian or her assistant for date stamping. This system should have worked well, except for the inevitable Stowbilly factor. A number of students would put a much different name on the card, from Haywood Jablome to Ben Dover. This would usually amount to a whole lot of nothing, since the books would be returned on time anyway and the name used on the card didn't really matter to the circulation assistant.

However, this flaw in the system did backfire spectacularly one day during study hall in the cafeteria. The Mole Lady herself came down from the library, which by Workman hallway standards probably took most of the morning, then approached one of the study hall monitors. She held a book card in one trembling hand, and in her inimitable craggy voice said "Attention, students, attention. We have an overdue book situation. Would Mr. JOHN please report to the library? Mr...ELTON... John?". We were all stunned. We didn't know whether to laugh or cry. She was completely sincere, and completely unaware that Elton John was a British singer-songwriter who had graduated years ago. Finally, someone shouted from the back of the room: "Elton's not here today, ma'am. He's on tour with Peter Frampton." Without missing a beat, the Mole Lady said "Well, would you please tell Mr. John to see me in the library when he gets back? It's very important that I speak with him." And then she was gone.

The original section of Workman was clearly built during a different time than my own. There were secrets around every corner, and most of them were inspired by the Red Menace scare of the 1950s. The small gym in the basement, which my predecessors often used as a makeshift dance hall during lunch, also served as an official atomic bomb shelter. A storage room connected to the gym still contained the remnants of emergency food supplies from the 1950s. There was also a tunnel which led from that storage room to the basement of the City Hall building. The City Hall building also had the iconic Civil Defense Shelter signs from the blissful "Duck and Cover" days. Considering the size of the student population at Workman and the capacity of the underground gym and bunker, there may have been a discussion or two in the day about who would get to enjoy the emergency rations and who would be toast during an actual atomic event.

The newer section of Workman housed many of the science classrooms, which meant access to Bunsen burners and a few serious chemicals. One of my favorite biology teachers was also an amateur bodybuilder, so his class lectures would often include the phrase "getting huge", followed by a Schwarzenegger-inspired pose or two. He would also perform experiments which were clearly not sanctioned by the school, but were usually fun to watch. One experiment involved pouring two liquid compounds together in a very tall glass cylinder. Nothing happened for a few minutes, but he explained that some chemicals generate significant heat when combined and we should just keep watching. A minute later, a steaming hot foam rose from the top of the cylinder, spilled over the side and flowed over the desk. The foam continued to slide along the floor and then out the classroom door.

What we may have called an exothermic reaction on the test soon became a smoldering pile of goo in the hallway.

The restrooms at Workman varied in overall quality and usability. The showers in the locker rooms were legendarily bad, followed closely by the student restrooms by the north entrance. In an effort to thwart smokers, the doors to each stall had been removed, which was not as much of a deal breaker on the boys' side as it was for the girls' side. Our assistant principal would periodically receive reports of illicit smoking in the girls room and throw a bucket of water through the front entrance. His actual smoker to poor girl just trying to brush her hair before class ratio was pretty abysmal, however. Other restrooms were much better, and the ones in the teachers' lounges were the best of all. This may explain why so many teachers went into apoplectic fits whenever a student wandered into the lounge by mistake. They were zealously protecting their pristine bathroom stalls, replete with working doors and abundant ashtrays.

They say all barely adequate but legally sufficient things must pass, and the Workman building was no exception. After the new 9th through 12th grade Stow-Munroe Falls High School became operational during the late 80s, the Workman building was generally abandoned. It would eventually be torn down, and the land would be converted for retail use. Many young Stowites would never guess an entire high school once stood on the property where Marc's is today. Many older Stowbillies, however, still remember running laps around the field behind the building, walking down to the public library after school, or hanging out at Eddie's bike shop or the Lawson's parking lot. The Workman building (and its surprisingly good cafeteria) may be gone, but many of us will miss that old Skinner box and its promise of better cheese to come.

LAKEVIEW HIGH SCHOOL:
Incidentally, No Lake and No View.

Somewhere between Kimpton's wild 60s architectural excesses and Workman's staple-as-you-go utilitarianism was Lakeview High School, the final 2 in Stow's clearly improvised 2-2-2 higher education plan. When Workman ceased to be workable as Stow's sole 9-12th grade high school, Lakeview became the "new" high school, thoughtfully located a quarter of a mile away from the existing one. There are those who still recall the day when the first class scheduled to graduate from Lakeview made its historic trek from Workman to the Lakeview campus. As the school yearbook would document, these pioneers weren't about to let a construction fence get in the way of educational progress, no sir.

Some of us Workmanites first experienced Lakeview as members of the marching band. Those freshmen and sophomore students would get off the buses at Lakeview and assemble on the practice field while the rest of us rode an additional quarter of a mile to Workman. Following band practice, there would be a parade of young band members walking to the Workman campus, while others made their way up to Lakeview for drivers' education classes. That walk between

Lakeview and Workman could either be a welcome break from the Skinner box or an object lesson on why others leave NE Ohio in droves during winter months. Since the class times did not always take into account the commute between campuses, most of us developed a walking pace somewhere between deliberate and alarmingly laser-focused.

Lakeview also featured a parking lot for both students and faculty, a situation which naturally cried out for a sense of law and order. The responsibilities of this position fell on one man and one man only, and that man had a name: One Bullet Barney, aka Rent-a-Cop. Barney indeed took his job very seriously, even if the driving student population did not. Getting past the Rent-a-Cop was the first step in a multi-step plan to get to McDonald's and back during the lunch period. The final step was getting back on campus while Barney was distracted by other student drivers working on step one. Getting a citation from Barney usually carried about as much weight as getting an overdue book notice from the Mole Lady at Workman, but few Stowbillies wanted to stay on his bad side for very long. He had a long memory, and a few friends still on the force.

Although the parking lot situation could be troubling at times, it paled in comparison to the vandalism magnet we euphemistically called the courtyard. The courtyard's centralized location and restricted access seriously harshed its buzz as a functional space, but it still served a purpose for senior classes during the last weeks of school. The aforementioned McDonald's restaurant had one thing every senior class hoped to capture, but only a handful ever did. Once every few years, a clearly disgruntled maintenance staff would have to fish a large fiberglass horse out of the courtyard, the same statue usually found in front of the Golden Arches of Stow. Sometimes a few crudities would be "painted" with bleach on the vulnerable courtyard grass, while at other times very large items would be dismantled and reassembled in the courtyard's confined space. If it was large and missing within five miles of Stow (especially during late May), searching in Lakeview's courtyard would not have been a bad idea.

Much like Kimpton's bucket of french fries or Workman's revered peanut butter bars, Lakeview's cafeteria had one feature that kept the faithful coming back for more. The standard lunch was generally satisfying, but for only an additional quarter students could stand in line for what was promoted as a chocolate milkshake. In retrospect, the fact that the milkshake mix was provided by the spoilsports at the USDA should have been a clue. It may not have been on a par with Friendly's or Stoddard's, but at least it was cold and creamy. Chocolaty, however, it was not. Nevertheless, many of us with two bits burning a hole in our pockets would dutifully stand in line all lunch period for a shot at natural dairy product goodness. The milkshake line also featured a few other snack items generally not found on the standard lunch menu, such as potato chips and candy bars. It was an alternative nation, a wink and a nod to nutritional mutiny in a lunchroom dedicated to the vagaries of the subsidized lunch program.

Lakeview during the early 80s was the site of a few other social experiments, like the ill-fated attempt to change the school's colors to pink and black and adopt a new mascot: The Stow High Good and Plentys. There were plenty of valid signatures on that petition, but unfortunately decades of maroon and gold tradition did not play in our favor. Another science project could be described as "one milk carton, one unused locker". After several months, the consensus among us scientists was that milk cartons were incredibly resilient, but things could only continue in one unfortunate direction. An unwashed gym shirt we named Fred Bread was also left in an unused locker for several months, but that experiment ended during a surprise locker inspection, which yielded a few illegal substances, some Playboy magazines and a green, fuzz-covered gym shirt. Fred Bread taught us a lot about living, about dying, and what it was to be a man. Actually, he taught us the value of a roll of quarters and a cup of laundry detergent.

One positive thing about the Lakeview campus was there was everything in a room and a room for everything. The building itself was almost a military-industrial complex in scope, with metal and wood shops, a massive gymnasium and locker rooms, band and choir rooms, business school rooms for IOE students, a darkroom for yearbook and newspaper photographers, not to mention offices for teachers and classrooms for everything from Latin to physics. The only catch was that students had five minutes at best to travel between all of those areas. Logistics rarely entered the equation whenever we were selecting our classes for the next semester. Anyone who signed up for Algebra II and choir, for example, would have to run from the last room of the top floor on the north side of the building to one of the last rooms on the bottom floor of the south side. The first bell served two purposes: the end of the class period, and the start of the daily 300 yard dash to the gym's locker room.

One class at Lakeview became very popular because of Ohio state law. A would-be driver under the age of 18 was required by law to present a certificate of completion from a recognized driver's ed school. Those who could afford the tuition fees had the option of attending what we liked to call a "crash course" on driving. Sear's offered a four day driver's ed course that satisfied at least the spirit of the law. Successful students would indeed receive a certificate of completion and could take their driving test in Cuyahoga Falls. However, there were many of us who enjoyed turning that kind of privileged positive into a Stowbilly negative. If a driver in the Stow area ever did something hazardous, like stopping short or failing to signal a turn, many of us would yell "Where did you learn to drive? SEARS?".

Meanwhile, the rest of us who were of driving age would sign up for the school-sponsored driver's ed course at Lakeview. This meant 18 weeks of classroom, simulator and real world training, but at least we wouldn't drive like those heathens with the Cracker Jack box certificates. The driver's ed instructor had exactly the demeanor you would expect from a social studies teacher shanghaied into teaching 16 years how to handle a 3,000 pound Deathmobile. He was fond of pointing out that he was a fervent bicyclist, so he was essentially giving us the means and ability to run him off the road later. We would watch the required "Blood Runs Red on the Highway" snuff films, spend time behind the wheel of a 1963 Studebaker in a driving simulator, then drive around town in a real car. The instructor did have a second brake installed on his side, however. At the end of the course, he doled out the certificates of completion, which he called "death certificates", and warned us all not to say anything approaching a thank you.

I'll end with one final memory of a teacher from Lakeview, a man who fought in Korea and enjoyed repeating his one good story about the place. It seems he was a hit with the local ladies because of his thick red hair, and they gave him a Korean nickname which he translated as "Number One Redhead". He taught history at Lakeview, although he was the kind of person I always thought should be *making* history somewhere else. I really enjoyed his class, and sometimes I would visit him during my 8th period study hall. He also owned a miniature golf course, so occasionally he would hand me a set of free passes to play a game or two. One day I walked into his empty classroom and found him watching TV. It wasn't a standard over-the-air channel, but an uncut cable movie channel. The cable television line ran on a pole right outside his classroom window, so he managed to splice some coaxial cable and tap into the signal. We watched Superman II for an entire class period, then I left to catch my bus. That's one of my lasting memories from my time spent at Lakeview High School, the building with no lake and no view, but still plenty of heart and soul.

HAVE THE SIRENS STOPPED SCREAMING, CLARICE? The Stow 4th of July Parade, Sponsored by Beltone.

The Victorians essentially perfected the Christmas holiday season, and the Puritans put a clear thumbprint on the celebration we now call Thanksgiving. However, the city of Stow OWNED the 4th of July; the competition was and still is for second place. Other cities may think they can assemble an acceptable bevy of Shriner midget cars, high school bands, beauty queens and themed floats, but when I was a child in the early 1970s, the Stow, Ohio Fourth of July parade operated on a completely different plane of existence. Route 59 through town became the epicenter of a 3 hour tribute to the civic duty gods.

The parade started assembling at the Stow-Kent Shopping Center, which was really the only location on that end of the street capable of supporting so many parade entrants. The parade route was one street running east to west, terminating at a review stand several miles away in the so-called downtown section of Stow. The mayor and other dignitaries would congregate at that review stand, but most of us regular folk would find a spot along Kent Road, pull out an old-school lawn chair and wait for clear signs of an impending parade. We usually didn't have to wait long. A few police officers on motorcycles would clear the stragglers off the street just before the largest peace time armada of emergency vehicles ever assembled started the festivities.

In the annals of historically bad ideas, one immediately springs to mind: Assembling a collection of fire trucks and ambulances from a three county area and having them drive single-file down the same stretch of densely populated highway. The CONCEPT of seeing a fleet of shiny fire trucks driving down our street sounded promising indeed to a 6 year old. However, the execution was a completely different story. As part of the parade ritual, all of these emergency vehicles decided to turn on their lights and sirens at the same time and for the same duration, which is to say, forever. The cumulative effect of all of those outside voices was a mind-numbing deafness, which lingered for the rest of the now-silent parade. To add audio insult to sonic injury, some of those fire engines also blew their diesel horns, which entered our bodies at the ear canal and exited out of places we forgot we had.

After the Beltone-sponsored parade of emergency vehicles passed by, life along the sidelines got a little easier. The American Field Service volunteers would walk up and down the parade route, hawking very small American flags that we would dutifully wave at the parade participants. For us kids, this was all leading up to the most important part of the parade: the candy toss. This was no small thing. Someone on a passing float would toss a handful of candy in our direction and a sugar-fueled feeding frenzy would begin. Every once in a while, an errant pitch would send the bulk of the candy in one direction and one direction only. Mine. Before I could pack up all of that Bubble Yum or Tootsie Roll booty, however, my mom would remind me of my Gallant tendencies and I'd end up redistributing it to the less fortunate. Darn the less fortunate.

One group that both scared and excited me was the Shriners, or as I thought of them, the old guys with the funny hats. At one point, their stunt vehicles of choice were Honda mini-bikes, which they would ride in intricate formations at different points along the route. Before going into their routine, however, a few of the flying monkey men would zip across the sidelines to make sure no groundlings were in the path of the mini-bikes. That little safety maneuver scared me to death, since I was often too busy picking up stray candy to notice a Shriner barreling down on top of me with 50 ccs of raw power behind him. The Shriners later switched to those miniature clown cars, which seemed to ratchet back the drama of non-athletic competition, in my younger opinion. You could only do so much damage in a clown car, and if these men thought riding mini-bikes designed for 8 year olds made them look like dorks on parade, the cars were not exactly babe wagons, either.

What happened next could only be described as an object lesson in terminal whiteness. The area high school bands would all march down the parade route in a stupefyingly predictable order: Majorettes, banner, drum major, band, band directors. Majorettes, banner, drum major, band, band directors. The upper funk limit for most of these bands was Stevie Wonder's "Sir Duke". Bands from Tallmadge, Hudson, Cuyahoga Falls, Kent and most notably, Stow, would take turns performing these squeaky tight Marvin the Martian arrangements of traditional march music and fight songs. Stow's fight song was the same as Ohio State's: "Across the Field" (alternative lyrics not included). Precision was the underlying theme, and for the most part we appreciated the homage to discipline and order. We were still Midwesterners, after all.

But nothing, NOTHING, prepared us for the volunteer drum corps from Akron. They wore purple and black uniforms, and clearly brought the funk from the county seat. No clarinets, no flutes, no saxophones; just trumpets and a boatload of drums. These guys didn't march in hyper-straight formations; they didn't really "march" at all. They eased on down the road with a solid BOOM-CHAKA-LAKA, BOOM-CHAKA-LAKA back beat driving them the whole way. As a young, frightened Caucasian, I had read the forbidden texts concerning funk, but during the Stow 4th of July parade, I actually had a chance to experience it in person. I liked it. I *really* liked it.

One of the more interesting, and one would think least innocent bystander-friendly, participants in the parade were the stunt shooters from Akron. At regular intervals along the route, a volunteer sitting in the back of an open-bed truck would hold out a balloon and shout "Fire!". At this point, the three trick shooters walking behind the truck would whip out their six-shooters and shoot the balloon dead. These people were lightning fast and extremely accurate, two qualities I admired in stunt shooters with live ammunition walking down a crowded street. I found out later that they only shot wax bullets, which would disintegrate on contact with the balloon. The version inside my eight-year-old mind was much better.

The floats were almost always from the "Red, White and Blaine" school of civic pride, and it was always interesting to see someone I knew from school or church strapped to one, but I noticed that some of my friends couldn't handle the pressures of sudden float fame. They would Bogart the candy, for one thing. After all we had been through from Kindergarten to July 3rd of that year, the least a buddy on a Stow Lions Club float could do was hook a brother up with that sweet, sweet Tootsie Roll action. Ingrates.

Perhaps nothing explains the Stowbilly psyche better than the ignoble end of all 4th of July parades. The parade participants who routinely gathered the most applause and adulation from the crowd weren't the high school bands, the gleaming and historical emergency vehicles or the local civic leaders. We saved our loudest cheers for the rows of street cleaners with their cheerfully waving drivers, who closed out the parade in style. Well, except for those of us who watched our last shot at Bazooka Joe and Dum Dums get swept away forever.

Your Well-Lit Public Space Or Mine?

The local FM talk radio station formerly known as WKNT changed its call letters to WNIR one year, and forever became known to Stowbillies as "Winner 100". The line-up of talk show hosts remained relatively unchanged, with the legendary Howie Chizek keeping most of the heat on during the day. At night, however, the airwaves belonged to a perennially optimistic radio host named Jim Albrecht and his "Dating Show". The Dating Show became 4 hours of the most riveting local radio ever produced, since there was every chance you knew either the caller or the prospective suitors personally. Although the host tried his best to enforce the first names only rule on air, there were always a few callers who inadvertently gave away the identity goods too soon, which in turn led to some serious ribbing at school the next week.

The Dating Show followed a relatively straightforward format. A candidate over the age of 18 would call the WNIR studio number, where he or she might speak with a producer before being put on hold for the actual show. The host would be given a few basic facts—Line 1 is Kerry, 27 years old, from Streetsboro—and he would proceed to chat with her on air for about 10 minutes or so. It was usually enough time for listeners to get the idea that she was a genuine contender and did not reek of desperation and Love's Baby Soft. After Jim and Kerry were through with the first interview, he would open the phone lines to prospective suitors. These callers presumably did NOT go through the same vetting process with a producer that Kerry did. These were often cold calls, with only a 5 second digital delay button standing between them and the general public. Jim would simply answer "Dating show", and the caller would make his pitch. Sometimes the clicking sound we heard was Jim killing out an obscenity-laced rant or adolescent callers who were clearly not in it to win it.

The legitimate callers would undergo one of Jim's patented one minute interrogations, in which he tried to suss out why this caller thought he was good enough to date his "daughter", who was still on hold but could hear everything. If the caller passed the initial sniff test, he would be put on hold while another caller went through the process. Eventually, there would be enough suitors on hold for Kerry to return to the conversation. She would talk to each caller individually, which was indeed every bit as uncomfortable and awkward as it sounds. Jim would then ask Kerry if she was interested in getting to know any of the callers better, and if she actually selected someone (not everyone did), they would exchange phone numbers off the air. This basic pattern continued for 4 more hours: Contestant, chat, callers, interrogation, decision, number exchange. Contestant, chat, callers, interrogation, decision, number exchange.

Because the Dating Show stayed on the air for so many years, it gained a cult following among the locals. We all had Dating Show stories to tell, either as contestants, callers, listeners or critics. The show really became more appealing when many of us migrated to the Kent State or Akron Zoo zip codes and discovered how difficult the adult dating scene could be. Suddenly calling a familiar voice and taking a chance on three strangers while on the radio didn't sound nearly as crazy as it once did. It was certainly no crazier than talking to a punk rock chick over a garbage burger at Jerry's Diner at 3 in the morning, or trying to compete with the Eurotrash dance music offerings at the Town House. At least the mission statement of the Dating show included the idea of actually connecting with someone else who was also at home listening to the radio on a Friday night.

One Dating Show story revolved around a contestant we shall call Denise. Denise was an older woman, with an engaging personality, a strong on-air presence and a somewhat husky voice. Jim chatted with

Denise for an unusually long time, which apparently gave Denise the courage to divulge something very personal about her life. At one point, Denise had been a man named Dennis. Dennis apparently had his Little Dennis surgically converted several years earlier, and Denise replaced Dennis on her driver's license. Jim allowed a few seconds of dead air to pass before responding to her with an uncharacteristically tepid "Oh...really?". The mental picture I had in my head was a switchboard filled with blinking lights suddenly going dark. The five second delay button got friction burns as Jim dutifully worked his way through the ineligible callers. Finally a few legitimate calls did get through and he was able to arrange an off-air number exchange between Denise and a man from the progressive city of Akron, Ohio. Jim would later say on air that he had his doubts about Denise and her claims of transsexualism. He became convinced "she" was a male prank caller who wanted to see how far he could go with the character before Jim hung up on him.

A few years later, the station set up a remote broadcast of the Dating Show at a restaurant near Akron. By now, Jim was a local institution, and a lot of former participants wanted to meet him to provide updates or whatever. That night, a woman came up to Jim during a commercial break and introduced herself as Denise. Yes, THAT Denise. She told Jim the date itself didn't work out, but the decision to appear on his show as Denise gave her the confidence to re-enter the dating world as a woman, not as a transvestite. She thanked Jim for treating her with respect, even after the awkward turn their original on air conversation took. Jim mentioned meeting Denise on a later show, noting that she was a very striking woman, and most people would never guess she once had a different set of equipment.

Some of the hook-ups arranged during the show took very bad turns in real life. Most were of the "now some creepy guy has my phone number" variety, but a few were more serious. This is one reason why the host and the producers of the Dating Show encouraged contestants to meet their blind dates at public locations and to use their best judgment when it came to future dates or the sharing of more personal information. The station itself could not be held liable for the actions of contestants or callers, so the show relied heavily on people playing nicely with each other. If things didn't work out after the first date, one person should go this way and the other one should go that way. Two ships and all that.

However, this wasn't always the case, and one night Jim nearly paid the ultimate price for introducing the wrong two people. Apparently the first date did not go well at all, since one of them was *not* a manic depressive psychopath with anger management issues. The other one decided that the Dating Show must pay for putting him together with a woman who did not drink his favorite brand of crazy juice. He called the WNIR studios in search of Jim Albrecht. The message was he was coming to kill him, and Hell was coming with him. Click. The station called several local law enforcement agencies, and they soon had enough information to identify the man and the car he was driving. Because this was all unfolding in real time, listeners would periodically call the station with updates. The car was now in Stow, the car was seen on 59, the car was in downtown Kent, etc. None of this information was of much comfort to Jim, who decided to host the show from underneath his desk that night.

Eventually the man and his car were detained on the road which led to the WNIR studio. The police discovered several empty bottles of alcohol and a loaded revolver in the vehicle. The man continued to issue threats against the Dating Show while being escorted to the Kent city jail. When news of the man's capture reached Jim, he thanked all of his listeners for their support and diligence and resumed his show after a longer than usual commercial break. For those of us listening to the drama unfold over the air, it was a useful object lesson on the hazards of setting up blind dates for a living.

The Dating Show format would eventually lose out to personal ads in tabloid newspapers for singles, then the much wider net of Internet dating websites like Match.com and Great Expectations. More single people wanted to know their potential dates had been professionally vetted, or at least provided legitimate information on their applications and profiles. The randomness and public scrutiny of a call-in radio dating show was no longer as appealing as it had once been, but for a few glorious years in the Stow area, Jim and WNIR did bring a lot of lonely people together, and that can only be a good thing.

Also by Michael Pollick

Michael Pollick's Proving Ground
Michael Pollick's Proving Ground
The Keepinnit Reels

9 798822 051905